This book
belongs to

Gracie Cho

CLIFFORD
THE BIG RED DOG®
Story and pictures by Norman Bridwell

SCHOLASTIC INC.

New York   Toronto   London   Auckland   Sydney   Mexico City   New Delhi   Hong Kong   Buenos Aires

ISBN 0-439-64491-7

12 11 10 9 8 7 6 5 4 3 2 1   4 5 6 7 8 9/0
Printed in the U.S.A.   24

First Scholastic printing, March 2004

For the real Emily Elizabeth

I'm Emily Elizabeth,

and I have a dog.

My dog is a big red dog.

Other kids I know have dogs, too.

Some are big dogs.

And some are red dogs.

But I have the biggest, reddest dog on our street.

This is my dog — Clifford.

We have fun together. We play games.

I throw a stick, and he
brings it back to me.

He makes mistakes sometimes.

We play hide-and-seek.

I'm a good hide-and-seek player.

I can find Clifford
no matter where he hides.

We play camping out,

and I don't need a tent.

He can do tricks, too.

He can sit up and beg.

Oh, I know he's not perfect.

He has some bad habits.

He runs after cars.

He catches some of them.

He runs after cats, too.

We don't go to the zoo anymore.

Clifford loves to chew on shoes.

And he digs up flowers, too.

It's not easy to keep Clifford.

He eats and drinks a lot.

His house was a problem, too.

But he's a very good watchdog.

And the mean boys don't come around anymore.

One day I gave Clifford a bath.

And I combed his hair
and took him to the dog show.

I'd like to say Clifford won first prize.

But he didn't.

I don't care.

You can keep all your small dogs.

You can keep all your black,

white, brown, and spotted dogs.

I'll keep Clifford. . . .

Wouldn't you?